Thomas the Tank Engine & Friends

A BRITT ALLCROFT COMPANY PRODUCTION

Based on The Railway Series by The Rev W Awdry
© Gullane (Thomas) LLC 2001

Visit the Thomas & Friends web site at www.thomasthetankengine.com

ISBN 0-439-33835-2

12 11 10 9 8 7 6 5 4 3 2 1   1 2 3 4 5 6/0
Printed in the U.S.A.
First Scholastic printing, October 2001

THOMAS and the Freight cars

by
The REV. W. AWDRY

SCHOLASTIC INC.

New York   Toronto   London   Auckland   Sydney
Mexico City   New Delhi   Hong Kong   Buenos Aires

Thomas used to grumble in the shed at night. "I'm tired of pushing coaches, I want to see the world."

The others didn't take much notice, for Thomas was a little engine who liked to talk big.

But one night, Edward came to the shed. He was a kind little engine and felt sorry for Thomas. "I've got some freight cars to take home tomorrow," he told Thomas. "If you take them instead, I'll push coaches in the yard."

"Thank you," said Thomas, "that will be nice."

So they asked their Drivers the next morning, and when they said, "Yes," Thomas ran happily to find the freight cars.

Now, freight cars are silly and noisy. They talk a lot and don't pay attention to what they are doing. They don't listen to their engine, and when he stops, they bump into each another screaming, "Oh! Oh! Oh! Oh! Whatever is happening?"

And, I'm sorry to say, they play tricks on an engine who is not used to them.

Edward knew all about freight cars. He warned Thomas to be careful, but Thomas was too excited to listen.

The shunter fastened the coupling, and when the signal dropped, Thomas was ready.

The Guard blew his whistle. *"Peep! Peep!"* answered Thomas and started off.

But the freight cars weren't ready. "Oh! Oh! Oh! Oh!" they screamed as their couplings tightened. "Wait, Thomas, wait." But Thomas wouldn't wait.

"Come—on.—Come—on," he puffed, and the freight cars grumbled slowly out from the siding onto the main line.

Thomas was happy. "Come along. Come along," he puffed.

"All—right!—Don't—fuss!—All—right!—Don't—fuss," grumbled the freight cars. They clattered through stations and rumbled over bridges.

Thomas whistled, *"Peep! Peep!"* and they rushed through the tunnel in which Henry had been shut up.

Then they came to the top of the hill where Gordon had gotten stuck.

"Steady now, steady," warned the Driver. He shut off the steam and began to put on the brakes.

"We're stopping, we're stopping," called Thomas.

"No! No! No! No!" answered the freight cars, bumping into each other. "Go—on!—Go—on!" And before his Driver could stop them, they had pushed Thomas down the hill, rattling and laughing behind him.

Poor Thomas tried hard to stop them from making him go too fast.

"Stop pushing, stop pushing," he hissed, but the freight cars would not stop.

"Go—on!—Go—on!" they giggled in their silly way.

He was glad when they got to the bottom. Then, ahead of him, he saw the place where they had to stop. "Oh, dear! What shall I do?"

They rattled through the station. Luckily, the line was clear as they swerved into the goods yard.

"Oo—ooh—e—r," groaned Thomas as his brakes held fast, and he skidded along the rails. "I must stop." And he shut his eyes tight.

When he opened them, he saw he had stopped just in front of the buffers, and there, watching him, was—Sir Topham Hatt!

"What are *you* doing here, Thomas?" he asked sternly.

"I've brought Edward's freight cars," Thomas answered.

"Why did you come so fast?"

"I didn't mean to, I was *pushed*," said Thomas sadly.

"Haven't you pulled freight cars before?"

"No."

"Then you've got a lot to learn about freight cars, little Thomas. They are silly things and must be kept in their place. After pushing them around here for a few weeks, you'll know almost as much about them as Edward. Then you'll be a Really Useful Engine."

14

Now flip the book over to start another Thomas & Friends adventure.

Thomas the Tank Engine & Friends

A BRITT ALLCROFT COMPANY PRODUCTION

Based on The Railway Series by The Rev W Awdry
© Gullane (Thomas) LLC 2001

Visit the Thomas & Friends web site at www.thomasthetankengine.com

ISBN 0-439-33835-2

12 11 10 9 8 7 6 5 4 3 2 1   1 2 3 4 5 6/0
Printed in the U.S.A.
First Scholastic printing, October 2001

THOMAS and the Breakdown Train

by
The REV. W. AWDRY

SCHOLASTIC INC.

New York   Toronto   London   Auckland   Sydney
Mexico City   New Delhi   Hong Kong   Buenos Aires

Every day Sir Topham Hatt came to the station to catch his train, and he always said "Hullo" to Thomas.

There were lots of freight cars in the yard—different ones came in every day—and Thomas had to push and pull them into their right places.

He worked hard—he knew now that he wasn't as clever as he had thought.

Besides, Sir Topham Hatt had been kind to him and he wanted to learn all about freight cars so he would be a Really Useful Engine.

But on a siding by themselves were some freight cars that Thomas was told he mustn't touch.

There was a small coach, some flat freight cars, and two strange things his Driver called cranes.

"That's the breakdown train," his Driver said. "When there's an accident, the workmen get into the coach, and the engine quickly takes them to help the hurt people and to clear and mend the line. The cranes are for lifting heavy things like engines, coaches, and freight cars."

One day, Thomas was in the yard, when he heard an engine whistling, "Help! Help!" A goods train came rushing through much too fast.

The engine (a new one named James) was frightened. His brake blocks were on fire, and smoke and sparks streamed out on each side.

"They're *pushing* me! They're *pushing* me!" he panted.

"On! On! On! On!" laughed the freight cars. Still whistling, "Help! Help!" poor James disappeared under a bridge.

"I'd like to teach those freight cars a lesson," said Thomas the Tank Engine.

Then a bell rang in the signal-box, and a man came running, "James is off the line—the breakdown train—quickly!" he shouted.

So Thomas was coupled on, the workmen jumped into their coach, and off they went.

Thomas worked his hardest. "Hurry! Hurry! Hurry!" he puffed. This time he wasn't pretending to be like Gordon, he really meant it.

Bother those freight cars and their tricks, he thought. I hope poor James isn't hurt.

They found James and the freight cars at a bend in the line. The brake-van and the last few freight cars were on the rails, but the front ones were piled in a heap. James was in a field with a cow looking at him, and his Driver and Fireman were feeling him all over to see if he was hurt.

"Never mind, James," they said. "It wasn't your fault, it was those wooden brakes they gave you. We always said they were no good."

Thomas pushed the breakdown train alongside the wreck. Then he pulled the unhurt freight cars out of the way.

"Oh—dear!—Oh—dear!" they groaned.

"Serves you right. Serves you right," puffed Thomas crossly.

When the men put the other freight cars on the line, he pulled them away, too. He was hard at work puffing backward and forward all afternoon.

"This'll teach you a lesson, this'll teach you a lesson," he told the freight cars, and they answered, "yes—it—will—yes—it—will," in a sad, groany, creaky sort of voice.

They left the broken freight cars and mended the line. Then, with two cranes, they put James back on the rails. He tried to move but he couldn't, so Thomas helped him back to the shed.

Sir Topham Hatt was waiting anxiously for them.

"Well, Thomas," he said kindly, "I've heard all about it, and I'm very pleased with you. You're a Really Useful Engine."

"James shall have some proper brakes and a new coat of paint. And you—you shall have a branch line all to yourself."

"Oh, Sir!" said Thomas happily.

Now Thomas is as happy as can be. He has a branch line all to himself and puffs proudly backward and forward with two coaches all day.

He is never lonely, because there is always an engine to talk to at the junction.

Edward and Henry stop by quite often and tell him the news. Gordon is always in a hurry and does not stop, but he never forgets to say, "*Poop, poop*" to little Thomas, and Thomas always whistles, "*Peep, peep*" in return.

Now flip the book over to start another Thomas & Friends adventure.